PUFFIN BOOKS

## OLIVER'S SECRET

Oliver Moffat is fed up. All his friends are going away and doing exciting things for the summer, and Oliver is stuck baby-sitting his five-year-old neighbour, Andrew.

But things are never as bad as they seem! Oliver *does* have the school gerbils to care for, and his pet-care business is booming! The trouble is he's only allowed to look after one pet at a time, and when more and more people ask him to look after their pets while they're away, he decides to keep them all hidden in the old garage behind his house. The result is pretty disastrous – and Oliver is not sure how long he can keep the secret from his mum!

Page McBrier has been an actress and a drama teacher. She is the author of twelve books and lives in Connecticut with her husband Peter and their two children.

D1340553

# PAGE McBRIER

# Oliver's Secret

*Illustrated by Blanche Sims*

PUFFIN BOOKS

PUFFIN BOOKS

Published by the Penguin Group
27 Wrights Lane, London w8 5TZ, England
Viking Penguin Inc., 40 West 23rd Street, New York, New York 10010, USA
Penguin Books Australia Ltd, Ringwood, Victoria, Australia
Penguin Books Canada Ltd, 2801 John Street, Markham, Ontario, Canada L3R 1B4
Penguin Books (NZ) Ltd, 182–190 Wairau Road, Auckland 10, New Zealand

Penguin Books Ltd, Registered Offices: Harmondsworth, Middlesex, England

First published in the USA by Troll Associates 1986
Published in Puffin Books 1989
1 3 5 7 9 10 8 6 4 2

Made and printed in Great Britain by
Richard Clay Ltd, Bungay, Suffolk
Filmset in Monophoto Baskerville

# CHAPTER

## I

Oliver Moffitt gave Pom-pom's lead a strong tug and hurried up Sutherland Avenue. 'Let's go,' he said. 'We'll be late.'

Pom-pom looked up at Oliver and whimpered.

'Oh, all right,' Oliver sighed. 'I suppose I can carry you.' He put the dog under his arm and took off at a run. 'I hope we haven't missed everyone.'

In one week school would be over for the summer. Oliver's classmates had all agreed to meet at the Quick Shoppe for an early celebration.

Oliver hurried around the corner. His friends Josh Burns and Matthew Farley were standing on the pavement. 'Hi,' Oliver waved. 'Where's everyone else?'

'Inside,' Matthew replied. He opened a packet of crisps and sat down on the kerb. 'I'll watch Pom-pom for you.'

'Thanks,' Oliver said. Pom-pom belonged to Oliver's mother, and Oliver walked him after school.

Jennifer Hayes and Kim Williams were standing at

the cash register. They were best friends. Oliver noticed that they'd changed from their school clothes into identical outfits. Jennifer was holding a large covered jar.

'Why are you wearing the same clothes?' he asked.

'We're twins today,' Jennifer replied.

Oliver shook his head. 'What's in the jar?'

'Gobstoppers,' said Jennifer. 'My grandmother sent them to me. I thought I'd pass them around.'

'Wow,' said Oliver. 'Your grandmother always sends you terrific things.' Oliver thought about his own grandmother. He hardly ever saw her. But he remembered how she sometimes smelled like apple pie, and that every year she sent him a cheque for his birthday.

Oliver bought a drink and a packet of biscuits and went back outside.

'Where's Sam?' he asked. Samantha Lawrence was Oliver's next-door neighbour and best friend. She was also the best athlete in his class.

'She had to go and get some camp clothes,' Kim said.

'Lucky Sam,' said Matthew. 'She's going to spend six whole weeks at summer camp.' He fed Pom-pom a crisp.

'Aren't you going to camp too?' Jennifer asked Matthew.

'I'm going on a computer course,' Matthew replied. 'Four mornings a week. My parents thought it would be a valuable experience.' Matthew threw a crisp in the air and caught it in his mouth. 'I'm going to have karate lessons in the afternoon, though. That should be fun.'

'I wish *I* could go on a computer course,' Josh said. Josh loved computers.

'Won't you be going to the lake?' Oliver asked Josh.

Josh nodded. 'It's brilliant up there,' he said. 'My brother and I swim all day long. Last summer we built a little dock to dive off.'

'The place we go in the summer has a lake and a dock too,' Kim chimed in. 'Our dock has a diving board on it. Jennifer's going to visit me, aren't you?' she said.

'Mm-huh,' Jennifer said. She had a gobstopper stuffed into each cheek.

'What are you doing this summer, Oliver?' Kim asked. 'Do you have any customers yet?'

Oliver was the only young person he knew who had his own pet-care business. Dogs and cats were his speciality, but he was also pretty good with gerbils, ducks and fish.

Oliver lived with his mother and Pom-pom. His mother worked as a bookkeeper for an insurance

3

agency. Oliver hadn't seen his father since he was a baby.

'No customers yet,' Oliver said. 'I'm trying to convince Mum to let me take the school gerbils.'

'Gerbils are really fun,' Matthew said.

'I think they're disgusting.' Jennifer shuddered. 'They look like baby rats.'

'They're quite sweet,' Kim said. 'I know someone who has a pet gerbil that escaped from its cage and was missing for a month. They finally caught it behind the refrigerator.'

'I would've left it there,' Jennifer said.

'Speaking of rats,' Josh said, 'look who's just showed up.'

Rusty Jackson, the school bully, screeched his bicycle to a stop.

'Watch it, shrimp,' he said to Matthew. 'You're blocking the door.'

Matthew quickly moved out of Rusty's way. He was the smallest kid in the class.

Rusty looked at the gang sitting on the kerb. 'What's this?' he said. 'A meeting of who's going to be thrown out of school?'

'You should talk, Rusty,' said Jennifer. Rusty was a couple of years ahead of them but had already been held back twice. Jennifer stood up and put the lid

back on her now-empty jar. 'Now that *you*'re here, I think I'll be going.'

'Me too,' said Kim.

Rusty pulled a plastic straw and some spitballs out of his pocket. He shot a few spitballs at a sign in the Quick Shoppe window that said FROSTIES SOLD HERE! The little wads of paper stuck to the window.

'You're disgusting,' said Jennifer. Rusty laughed.

'Hey, Jennifer,' he said. 'I hear you're going to be around all summer. Maybe I can show you how to shoot spitballs.'

Jennifer made a face and ran out of the car park. 'Stay away from me, Rusty!' she shouted.

'What are you staring at?' Rusty asked Josh.

'Nothing,' said Josh.

Rusty laughed and walked into the shop.

'Just my luck,' said Oliver with a sigh. 'The only two people who'll be around all summer are Jennifer and Rusty. Some summer.'

'Mum,' said Oliver during supper, 'why aren't we going away this summer?'

Mrs Moffitt looked at Oliver and smiled. 'Who's going to pay the bills while we're on holiday?' she asked.

'But everyone else from school is doing something fun this summer,' Oliver said. 'Matthew is going on a

6

computer course and having karate lessons. Josh and Kim are staying at lakes. Sam is going to summer camp.'

'You're going to have fun next door at Andrew's house,' said Mrs Moffitt.

'What's so great about staying with a five-year-old?'

'Mrs Finch is counting on your help,' said Mrs Moffitt. 'Especially since she has a new baby.'

Oliver looked at his mother and rolled his eyes.

'Oliver,' said his mother, 'right now we can't afford special classes or camp. Mrs Finch is doing us a big favour by looking after you.'

Oliver sighed. 'I know,' he said. 'But can't I at least take care of the school gerbils?'

Mrs Moffitt smiled gently. 'Oliver, you know how much gerbils upset Pom-pom.'

Pom-pom looked up at Mrs Moffitt and whined.

'But Mum,' said Oliver, 'I'm the only person in my class who has nothing to do all summer. Can't I have *one* customer? I know all about gerbils. They're easy to take care of. You just feed them once a day and they keep their cage really clean.'

Mrs Moffitt didn't answer.

Oliver took a few green beans and dropped them on to his mashed potatoes. He pretended his last bite of chicken was an army tank. He moved the tank towards the green beans with his fork.

7

'I've got a good idea,' Oliver said. 'What if I cleaned out the garage? We could keep the gerbils out there, away from Pom-pom.'

'I don't think so, Oliver,' said Mrs Moffitt.

'But there's an awful lot of old junk out there,' Oliver continued. 'You can't even fit the car in.'

Mrs Moffitt sighed. 'Why don't you finish your supper?' she said. 'I'll think about it.'

The next day, Oliver and Sam were walking home from school.

'Has your mum decided about the gerbils yet?' Sam asked.

'She's still thinking it over,' Oliver replied.

'What about Andrew?' said Sam.

'Mum says if I keep an eye on Andrew, Mrs Finch will keep an eye on me.'

'Andrew is impossible,' said Sam. 'Remember when he painted your mum's car with red nail polish? His mother didn't even spank him.'

'I know,' Oliver replied glumly. 'Maybe he'll be sick all summer and have to stay in his room. Every time he comes over to my house, he breaks something.'

Sam stopped at the corner. 'Want to go to Huff's Antiques with me?' she asked. 'I'm looking for a birthday present for Pam, my camp friend. She collects china animals.'

Oliver had never been inside Huff's Antiques before. Everything in there was really old – especially Mr Huff.

'Wow,' said Oliver. 'This looks like our garage.'

Sam led him over to a display case. 'Pam likes horses,' she said. 'Look for any horses.'

The case had three long shelves. Oliver peered at each object on the top shelf. 'Look!' he pointed.

'Have you found a horse?' Sam asked.

'No,' said Oliver. 'But see that heart-shaped locket on the chain? My mum used to have one just like it. She lost it a long time ago. It was her favourite.'

'It's really pretty,' Sam said. 'Maybe you can surprise her with this one. How much is it?'

Mr Huff opened the display case with a key. He picked the locket up and held it near his eyes. 'Eight pounds,' he said.

Oliver's heart sank. 'Thank you,' he said. 'I just can't afford it,' he whispered to Sam. 'Mum would have loved it.'

'Maybe you can save up the money,' Sam said. 'Does your mum have a birthday coming up?'

'At the end of the summer,' Oliver replied. He thought for a minute. 'I can try earning the money.'

'What about getting more customers?' suggested Sam.

'No way,' Oliver replied. 'Mum isn't sure about

letting me keep the gerbils. And she has a rule: only one customer at a time.'

'Well, maybe you can think of something else,' said Sam.

'I know she'd really like that locket,' Oliver said.

Oliver sat in his bedroom that night, thinking. There had to be a way to get that locket. But even if his mother let him keep the gerbils, he still wouldn't have quite enough. He heard a knock on the door.

'Am I interrupting anything?' said Mrs Moffitt.

'No, Mum,' said Oliver.

'I've been thinking about your offer,' Mrs Moffitt said. 'Maybe the school gerbils wouldn't be too much trouble – if you kept them in the garage.'

Oliver jumped out of his chair and gave his mother a big hug. 'Thanks, Mum!' he said. 'I promise I'll take good care of them. And you won't believe how neat the garage will look.'

Mrs Moffitt smiled. 'You still have Pom-pom to take care of first,' she said. 'I'm counting on you to do a good job.'

Oliver grinned. 'No problem, Mum,' he said. 'What can go wrong with a few gerbils?'

Oliver wiped a bead of sweat off his forehead and carefully backed out of the garage door. A very tall lamp wobbled in his arms. 'Andrew!' he shouted. 'Where are you? I need your help.'

Something went crashing inside the garage. Oliver put down the lamp.

Andrew came running out. 'Mummy!' he screamed. 'I want Mummy.'

'Are you OK?' asked Oliver.

Andrew stopped screaming and nodded his head.

'Mummy is busy with your baby sister, Nicole, remember?' Oliver said. 'You're supposed to be helping *me* right now.'

Andrew looked at Oliver.

Oliver sighed. This had been going on all morning. 'What's the matter?' he asked. 'What was that crash?'

Andrew burst into tears.

'Let's go and look,' said Oliver. They walked into the garage. 'See?' said Oliver, pointing. 'It's only the rubbish bin. It must have fallen over.'

'I'm hungry,' Andrew wailed. 'Can we go to your house for lemonade?'

'Why don't you help me finish clearing out this corner first? And have you fed the gerbils their sunflower seeds yet?'

Andrew nodded.

Oliver wondered if Sam had arrived at camp yet. She had left on the train yesterday afternoon. Lucky Sam.

Oliver could feel Andrew pulling on his shirt. 'Now what?' he said.

'Let's go and play with Pom-pom,' Andrew said.

'Not now,' Oliver replied. 'Let's finish the garage first.'

'Andrew! Oliver!' called Mrs Finch.

'It's my mummy!' screamed Andrew. He disappeared through the hedge.

'Psst! Oliver!'

A voice was coming from the bushes.

'Who is it?' Oliver asked.

'It's Tim B.,' said the voice. Tim B. poked his head through the bushes. 'Can I talk to you for a minute?'

Tim B. was in Oliver's class at school. Although he'd been at Oliver's school for two years, hardly anyone knew him well. He was very quiet and kept to himself.

'Hi, Tim,' said Oliver. 'What's up?'

Tim B. looked as if he was about to cry. He motioned Oliver into the bushes. On the ground was a cardboard box.

'What's in there?' Oliver asked.

Tim opened the box carefully.

'Hey,' said Oliver, 'it's an aquarium. Is it yours?'

Tim nodded.

'I never knew you had an aquarium,' said Oliver. He looked closer. 'Wow. This aquarium is full of fish!'

13

he exclaimed. 'Tetras, oscars, angelfish — it must weigh a ton. What's it doing in the bushes?'

'My family is going away for the summer,' Tim said. 'If I can't find anyone to take care of the fish, I'll have to give them away.'

'Don't do that,' said Oliver. 'This is a great aquarium. I'm sure you'll find someone.'

'I was hoping *you* could look after them,' said Tim.

Oliver shook his head. 'Gosh, I'd really like to have your fish, but I can't. I told my mum I'd only take care of one pet. And I've already got the school gerbils.'

'You don't understand,' said Tim. 'You're my last chance. I've asked everyone I can think of. We leave this afternoon.' He pulled some money out of his pocket. 'This is all the money I have. I hope it's enough.'

Oliver looked at the money and shook his head again. 'I don't know,' he said. 'A rule is a rule. I don't think I should.'

Tim bent down and watched the fish swim around in the tank. 'I've had some of these fish for three years,' he said sadly. 'They're my friends. Maybe Perkins' Pet Supply will buy them back from me.'

Oliver felt terrible for Tim. He thought about the space he'd cleared out in the garage. Maybe there was room for the aquarium in there. Fish were very quiet. His mother would never know. Besides, he could use the extra money to help buy his mother the locket.

'Tim, I've changed my mind. I'll be glad to take your fish.'

'You will?'

'Yes,' said Oliver. 'After all, what are a few fish? Just help me move them into the garage.'

A few minutes later, Tim and Oliver were moving an old chest of drawers next to the table with the gerbil cage.

'Lewis and Clark will love having these tropical fish for neighbours,' Oliver said, looking at the two gerbils. 'It'll help to keep them occupied.' He got down on his hands and knees. 'Let's plug the aquarium in before the fish get any colder,' he said.

Oliver set the aquarium on top of the chest. He crawled under it to look for a socket.

'What are you doing, Oliver?' asked Andrew.

Oliver jumped and banged his head on the chest. He'd forgotten about big-mouth Andrew. If Andrew knew about the aquarium, he'd be sure to tell his mother.

Oliver thought fast. 'Hi, Andrew,' he said. He stood up quickly to block the aquarium from Andrew's view.

'Nice fishy,' said Andrew, pointing behind Oliver's back.

'Andrew,' said Oliver, 'do you know what a secret is?'

Andrew nodded.

Oliver motioned him to come closer. 'Do you think you're old enough to keep a very important secret?' he whispered.

Andrew smiled. 'Is it the fishies?' he said, peeking around Oliver's back.

Oliver shrugged. 'Maybe,' he said. He looked at Tim and winked. 'Would you take the secret oath?'

Andrew jumped up and down. 'I would! I would!' he shouted. 'Tell me the secret.'

'Follow me,' Oliver said. He led Tim and Andrew out of the garage and up to his room. After shutting the door, Oliver closed the curtains and turned off the light. The room was dark.

'Wait here,' Oliver whispered. He went out and came back a few seconds later with a glass of water and an old towel. Oliver draped the towel over Andrew's head.

'What are you doing?' Andrew asked.

'Shhh,' said Oliver. 'You're about to be initiated into the secret-keepers' club.'

He grabbed his torch from his desk drawer and shone it into Andrew's eyes.

'Ow,' said Andrew, squinting.

'Quiet,' warned Oliver. He took his prized stuffed

owl off his desk. 'Put your hand on the owl's head,' Oliver said.

Andrew did as he was told.

'Now, repeat after me,' said Oliver. 'I, Andrew Finch, do solemnly promise not to mention the aquarium in the garage.'

Andrew repeated the vow.

Oliver sprinkled a couple of drops of water on Andrew's head. 'Hubba, dubba, hubba. You are now my special pet-care assistant,' he said.

Andrew pulled the towel off his head. 'Yippee!' he shouted. Then he said, 'Oliver? What's a quarium?'

'That's one word – aquarium,' Tim said. 'It's a glass tank for keeping fish.'

'Oh,' said Andrew. 'Then the secret *is* the fishies.'

Oliver sighed. 'We're not finished yet,' he said, pushing Andrew back down. Andrew sat very still. 'I hope you understand. If you breathe one word of this to ANYONE, you won't be allowed in the garage ever again.'

'I promise,' Andrew whispered.

'Good,' said Oliver. 'Now you can go.'

Andrew tore down the stairs. Tim looked after him.

'Oliver,' said Tim. 'That was great. I really appreciate this.'

'No problem,' said Oliver. 'Your fish are in good hands with Oliver Moffitt.'

# CHAPTER

## 2

'Oliver,' said Mrs Moffitt a few nights later, 'how are the gerbils working out?'

Oliver was lying on the living-room floor watching TV. 'Fine, Mum,' he said. 'They're really happy out in the garage.'

'When can I see all the hard work you've been doing?' she asked.

Oliver sat up quickly. 'Uh, any time,' he said.

'How about now?' Mrs Moffitt smiled.

Oliver gulped. 'Fine,' he said. 'But give me a few minutes to straighten up. I left the gerbil food on the floor and I don't want you to trip over it.'

Oliver dashed out to the garage. In one minute, he had shoved the chest of drawers back behind an old sofa. He draped a pink bedspread over the aquarium.

There was a knock on the door. 'Mind if I come in?' said Oliver's mother.

'No,' said Oliver. His heart was racing. 'Have a look around,' he said casually.

Mrs Moffitt smiled and nodded her head. 'It looks

so neat in here,' she said. 'I knew I could count on you.'

Oliver smiled.

The next morning, Oliver got up earlier than usual. He'd dreamed about fish and gerbils all night. 'Might as well have some breakfast,' he said to himself.

He tiptoed downstairs and ate a bowl of cereal. It was seven o'clock. His mother and Pom-pom didn't wake up until seven-thirty. Oliver slipped out of the back door.

As soon as he got to the garage, he noticed a large cardboard box in front of the door. That's funny, he thought. I don't remember leaving the box there.

The box moved.

'Uh-oh,' he said. He ran over and tore open the lid.

'Oh, no!' Oliver said. Inside the box was a litter of black-and-tan guinea pigs, squirming around on an old towel. A handful of lettuce sat in the corner of the box. Taped to the side of the box was a note: 'I heared you take care of pets. Pleez watch my ginee pigs.' The note was not signed. Oliver wondered who had left the babies.

'Poor things,' Oliver muttered. 'Six,' he said aloud. '*Six* of them.'

Oliver could hear Mrs Moffitt calling him. 'Coming, Mum,' he said.

He dragged the box into the garage and put it on

I heared you take care of pets. pleez watch my ginee pigs.

the table next to the gerbils. 'Don't worry,' he told
the guinea pigs. 'Everything will be OK.'

As soon as Mrs Moffitt left for work, Oliver phoned
Matthew.

'How's it going?' Matthew said. 'Are you having
fun with Lewis and Clark?'

Oliver told Matthew about Tim B.'s aquarium and
the new guinea pigs.

'And your mum doesn't know about any of them?'
Matthew asked.

'No,' said Oliver. 'She'd probably kill me if she
found out.'

'What are you going to do?' asked Matthew.

'I suppose I'll just have to keep the guinea pigs
until they're big enough to give away,' Oliver said. 'I
have to live up to my pet-care reputation. I can't just
abandon them. Besides, they're really sweet.'

'Good luck,' said Matthew. 'Let me know if you
need any help. Maybe I can come and visit you after
my computer course.'

'Any time,' said Oliver.


Oliver was about to go into the garage when Andrew
appeared. 'How's my assistant?' Oliver asked.

Andrew smiled and gave the thumbs-up sign.

'Since you're so good at keeping secrets, I have
another one for you,' said Oliver.

Andrew's eyes lit up as he followed Oliver into the garage.

'These are guinea pigs,' Oliver said. 'Can you still keep a secret?'

Andrew nodded.

'I hope so,' said Oliver. 'Now go to my fridge and get all the celery and lettuce you can find. We'll chop it up for the gerbils and guinea pigs.'

'Oliver,' said Mrs Moffitt when she came home, 'do you know what happened to the celery and lettuce? I wanted to make a salad for supper.'

Oliver walked over and looked in the vegetable bin. 'There's none left?' he said.

Mrs Moffitt put her hands on her hips. 'I know *you* didn't eat it all, Oliver. I can barely get you to finish your salad.'

Oliver nodded. 'Right,' he said.

'Well?' said Mrs Moffitt.

'Andrew must have eaten it,' said Oliver.

'A whole head of lettuce and celery?'

'You know how he likes to have snacks,' said Oliver. 'I asked him to feed a little bit to the gerbils, and he must have fed the rest to himself.'

Mrs Moffitt frowned. 'I'll have to say something to Linda Finch,' she said. 'Too much of any one food is very bad for a young child.'

'Right,' said Oliver.

After dinner, Oliver sat in his room. He tried to work out how much it would cost to keep the guinea pigs. The extra food was really going to cut into his profits. He covered page after page with arithmetic, then shook his head. 'There's no way I can buy that locket now,' he said. 'I'll have to work out another way to earn the money.'

Oliver's phone rang. 'Pet care,' he said as he picked it up.

'It's Kim,' said the voice at the other end. 'How's business?'

'Great,' said Oliver. 'Busier than ever.'

'How would you like another customer?' Kim asked.

Oliver took a deep breath and looked at the papers on his desk. 'What kind of customer?' he asked.

'It's my rabbit, Hopkins,' said Kim. 'Our neighbour was supposed to take care of him, but she's just found out she's allergic to Angora rabbit fur.'

Oliver drummed a pencil on his desk. 'I don't know . . .'

'I'm willing to pay the going rate,' said Kim. 'Besides, I'd rather *you* looked after Hopkins than Hermann's Pet Palace.'

Oliver looked over his arithmetic again. With another paying customer, he'd be able to feed the guinea pigs and still save enough to buy his mother the locket. It was tempting.

'O K,' he said suddenly. 'I'll do it. Meet me outside our garage tomorrow at eleven.'

'Thanks a lot, Oliver,' said Kim. 'You don't know how much I appreciate this.'

'No problem,' said Oliver. 'Hopkins shouldn't be any trouble.'

Oliver and Andrew were busy all the time now. After the morning feeding, Oliver and Andrew took Pompom for a walk. Pom-pom didn't know about the pets in the garage, and Oliver meant to keep things that way. Pom-pom would have gone crazy with jealousy.

After Oliver and Andrew returned from their walk, Oliver put Hopkins in the back garden for exercise. Andrew and Hopkins chased each other around until lunchtime.

Mrs Finch was a pretty good cook. She never made Andrew eat anything he didn't like. Most of the time they had peanut-butter-and-banana sandwiches, cinnamon toast and homemade chocolate-chip cookies. Oliver always got his choice of chocolate- or strawberry-flavoured milk.

Andrew was working out better than Oliver had planned. In another week or so, Andrew would know how to clean out all the cages by himself. Oliver could sit back and relax.

One morning Oliver was busy chopping up lettuce when Andrew came running over.

'We need more lettuce for the baby gerbils,' Andrew said.

'Andrew,' Oliver replied, 'those are baby *guinea pigs*, not gerbils.'

Andrew shook his head. 'Gerbils,' he insisted. 'Come on. I'll show you.'

Oliver and Andrew walked over to the gerbil cage. 'See?' Andrew pointed. '*These* are gerbils. Four little baby gerbils.' Oliver looked inside the cage and gasped.

'How could this happen?' he said. 'I thought we had two males.'

Andrew banged on the glass cage and tried to get the mother gerbil's attention.

'Don't do that,' Oliver said. 'You'll scare the babies.' Oliver checked to make sure all the gerbils were OK.

'Where will we put the babies?' Andrew wanted to know.

'They don't need to be separated from their mother for about three weeks,' Oliver replied. He looked around the garage. 'It's getting pretty crowded in there, though.' He sighed. 'I suppose we should clear out some more space. Besides, the guinea pigs have outgrown the cardboard box.'

Oliver and Andrew spent most of the afternoon moving cartons and furniture around the garage.

'Look,' said Andrew. He held up an old bucket. 'We can put the baby gerbils in here when they get big enough.'

'Good idea,' said Oliver. 'See if you can find anything else. We need at least two more cages.'

Oliver opened the garage door as wide as he could. 'Let's put some of this old stuff out on the lawn until we can clear some more space,' he said.

Andrew nodded and started pulling some cardboard boxes on to the lawn.

By late afternoon the lawn was crowded with junk. 'I hope we have time to get all this put away before Mum gets home,' said Oliver. Andrew wasn't much of a help when it came to tidying things.

'Hey, Oliver, are you having a garage sale?' someone called. It was Rusty.

'Hello,' said Oliver crossly. The last person he wanted to see was Rusty Jackson. Oliver picked up one end of an old trunk and dragged it across the yard.

Rusty got off his bicycle and looked around. 'You selling any of this stuff?' he asked.

'I'm just cleaning out the garage,' Oliver said.

Rusty continued to poke around.

'Hey,' said Oliver, 'this is private property.'

'I'm not bothering anyone,' Rusty replied. He walked over to a blue bicycle with orange rust spots. 'Is this for sale?' he asked.

'It belongs to my mother,' Oliver said.

'Since when has your mum ridden a bike?' Rusty hooted.

Oliver squirmed uncomfortably. 'It must have been a couple of years,' he answered.

'What if I buy it from you?' Rusty said. He climbed on to the bicycle and flexed the hand brakes.

'It's not really mine,' said Oliver.

'Come on,' Rusty said. 'Your mum never uses it. It's a piece of junk.' He pulled some money out of his pocket and waved it in Oliver's face. 'What do you say?'

Oliver thought about Rusty's offer. Now that he had more gerbils, he could use Rusty's money. It could buy another cage and extra food. He'd still have enough to buy the locket too. Oliver peered into the garage. That bicycle took up an awful lot of room. His mother would never know it was missing.

'Sold,' said Oliver.

Rusty grinned and handed him the money. 'Thanks, pal,' he said. 'You've got yourself a deal.'

Oliver ate three helpings of tuna casserole at supper that night.

'What did you do all day?' said Mrs Moffitt. 'I've never seen you eat so much.'

'It's tough keeping an eye on Andrew,' Oliver said. He started to take a fourth helping.

'Please leave a bite for Pom-pom,' said Mrs Moffitt. 'This is his favourite supper.'

Oliver put a spoonful on a saucer and stuck it under the table.

'I'm so happy you and Andrew are getting along,' said Mrs Moffitt. 'Linda says that Andrew adores you.'

'Andrew is O K.'


One afternoon Matthew stopped by on his way to karate lessons. Oliver was sitting in the garden with Hopkins. He was reading a book called *Animals of the African Plains*. Andrew was busy changing the sawdust in the gerbils' and guinea pigs' cages.

'Let me give you the tour,' Oliver said. He let Matthew hold Hopkins as they walked through the garage.

'This is really terrific, Oliver,' said Matthew. 'You practically have a zoo here.'

Oliver smiled proudly.

'Can we take the guinea pigs outside?' asked Matthew.

'Yes,' Oliver replied. 'Let's put Hopkins back in his cage first.'

Just then Andrew ran over. 'Can I play with the fishies now?' he asked.

'Have you finished all your chores?' said Oliver.

Andrew nodded.

'OK,' said Oliver. 'But don't tap on the glass or stick your hands in the water. Just watch them.'

One minute later Andrew came running outside again. 'A big fish is eating all the little fish!' he screeched.

'Don't be ridiculous,' said Oliver. 'The fish are just playing.'

Andrew shook his head. 'No,' he said. 'I saw it.'

Oliver looked at Matthew and chuckled. 'Sometimes Andrew imagines things,' he said.

Matthew stood up and put the guinea pig back in the box.

'Where are you going?' asked Oliver.

'I think we should make sure,' said Matthew. He had an aquarium at home.

'If you say so,' said Oliver. The three boys walked over to the aquarium.

'See?' Andrew pointed.

'Oh, my gosh!' said Matthew. 'He's right. We need to separate these fish right away!'

'Do we?' said Oliver.

Andrew ran into Oliver's house and returned with a big glass bowl.

'That's my mother's casserole dish,' said Oliver.

'Not any more,' said Matthew. He took the bowl from Andrew and carefully filled it with water from the fish tank. 'If we don't take the babies out, the mother will eat them all. I have to do this whenever my fish have babies.'

'Babies?' said Oliver. 'We have *fish* babies now?'

Andrew clapped his hands together and jumped up and down. 'More babies!' he said. 'Hooray!'

'Where will we put them?' said Oliver. 'They can't stay in the casserole dish.'

'I can lend you an extra aquarium,' said Matthew. 'I keep one for emergencies like this.'

Oliver looked at the casserole dish and groaned. 'Look at all those baby tetras,' he said. 'There must be a million.' He sighed. 'I think I'd better take another trip to Perkins's. Maybe the babies would like some freeze-dried worms.'

'I'll drop off the aquarium tomorrow morning before my computer course,' said Matthew.

'Thanks,' was all Oliver could say.

'How was your day?' Mrs Moffitt asked at supper.

'Fine,' said Oliver. He felt really exhausted.

Mrs Moffitt looked at Oliver and smiled. 'Oliver,' she said, 'I really appreciate how helpful and co-operative you've been all summer.'

'No problem,' said Oliver.

Mrs Moffitt smiled again. 'I have a big surprise for you,' she said.

Oliver looked up from his supper.

'Since you've been so good and patient,' said Mrs Moffitt, 'I've decided that you've earned a holiday.'

'Have I?' said Oliver.

'Yes!' exclaimed Mrs Moffitt. She rose from her chair and gave Oliver a big hug. 'Guess what. We're going to the seaside for a week! I've made reservations at a wonderful old hotel. We'll be able to swim, go for long walks and ride our bikes along the beach.'

'Our bikes?' said Oliver.

'Yes,' said Mrs Moffitt. 'Remember that old bike I've got in the garage?'

'Oh,' Oliver replied. He thought he was going to choke.

Mrs Moffitt gave Oliver another hug. 'We haven't had a real holiday for years,' she said. 'We're going to have a wonderful time.'

Oliver smiled as best he could. 'Wow, Mum,' he said. 'That sounds great. How soon do we leave?'

# CHAPTER
## 3

Oliver rode his bicycle over to Rusty's house the next morning as soon as his mother had left for work.

'Hello, Mrs Jackson,' he said. 'Is Rusty at home?'

'He's out in the garage, dear,' she said.

Oliver walked around to the back of the house. He could hear a lot of pounding and hammering.

'Hello,' Oliver called. 'Anybody here?' Oliver looked into the garage and gasped. There was Rusty, kneeling on the floor with a huge monkey wrench. All around him was Mrs Moffitt's bicycle. It was scattered across the garage floor in what seemed like a million pieces.

'Oh, no!' Oliver cried. 'What have you done to Mum's bike?'

'What does it look like?' Rusty said. 'I took it apart.' He picked up the monkey wrench and started to pull Mrs Moffitt's front tyre off its rim.

'Wait!' Oliver yelled.

Rusty put the wrench down. 'What's the matter?' he asked.

Oliver took a deep breath. 'I want to buy this bicycle back,' he said.

Rusty's expression turned into a sinister grin. 'No problem,' he said. He picked up a huge plastic bag and swept in all the parts. Then he handed the bag to Oliver. 'Here you are.'

Oliver felt sick. He had no idea how to put the bicycle back together. 'I wanted to buy it back all in one piece,' he said.

'Well, I can put it back together for you,' Rusty said, 'but it will cost you extra.'

'How much extra?' Oliver said weakly.

Rusty named his price.

'But that's three times what you paid for it!' Oliver exclaimed. 'I haven't got that much money.'

Rusty shrugged and turned the bag upside down. The bicycle parts clattered back on to the garage floor. 'Take it or leave it,' he said. 'Putting a bike together is hard work.' He picked up the wrench and the front tyre again.

Oliver grabbed Rusty's arm. 'Stop!' he said.

Rusty looked up.

'I need some time to get the money together,' Oliver said quickly.

Rusty put his wrench down. 'OK,' he said. 'I'll give you two days.'

'That's not enough time!' Oliver protested. 'How about a week?'

Rusty shook his head. 'Sorry,' he said, giving Oliver his most awful grin. 'I'll tell you what. If you can't get the cash, I'd be willing to strike a bargain. How about this bike for your stuffed owl?'

Oliver groaned. The stuffed owl was his most prized possession. He'd won it during last year's science fair. Ever since then Rusty had been trying to take it away from him.

Oliver knew he was cornered. 'OK,' he said desperately. 'If I can't get the cash, you can have the owl.'

'It's a deal,' said Rusty. 'See you in two days.'

When Oliver got back to his house, Andrew was in the garage feeding the animals. At least one thing is still going right, Oliver thought.

Andrew came racing outside. 'Guess what!' he said. 'More baby gerbils!'

Oliver put his hand to his head. 'I don't believe this,' he said. 'What next?'

'No problem, Oliver,' said Andrew. 'I've already put them in the casserole dish.'

Oliver sighed. 'That's just great,' he said. 'First fish and now gerbils. If Mum ever knew how many animals have lived in that dish, we'd never eat tuna casserole again.' He walked into the garage to see the new babies.

'How many this time?' he asked.

'Six,' said Andrew proudly.

Oliver counted on his fingers. 'That's twelve gerbils, six guinea pigs, two tanks of tropical fish, and a rabbit.' He sighed again. 'Help me move this furniture around, Andrew,' Oliver said finally. 'It looks as if we need some more room in here again.'

That evening Oliver sat in his office trying to work out how to earn enough money to buy back his mother's bicycle. He had to put the bicycle back in the garage soon. He and his mother would leave for the beach in just two weeks.

Mrs Moffitt called to him from downstairs.

'What is it?' Oliver called back.

'Have you seen the casserole dish?' she asked. 'I've searched everywhere for it.'

'Uh, not recently,' Oliver replied. He frantically looked around his room for something else to put the gerbils in. Oliver spotted his waste-paper basket. 'Perfect,' he said. He dumped all the rubbish on his desk and ran downstairs.

Mrs Moffitt was kneeling on the kitchen floor with her head stuck inside a cabinet. 'I know it's here somewhere,' she muttered.

'I'll be back in a minute, Mum!' Oliver said. He ran out to the garage and turned on the light. The mother gerbil was busy feeding her babies. Oliver poured some fresh sawdust into the waste-paper basket, then carefully moved the gerbils from the casserole dish into it. 'That should keep you happy for a while,' he said. He gave the mother gerbil a few sunflower seeds as an extra treat.

Oliver ran back to the kitchen with the casserole dish. His mother still had her head buried in the cabinet.

'Look what I've found, Mum,' he said. 'It was in the garden. Andrew must have used it to give Pompom a drink. I'll have to remind him that this dish is only for cooking.'

Mrs Moffitt smiled. 'Where would I be without your help?' she said.

Oliver lay awake for a long time that night. How was he going to get back his mother's bicycle? And how was he going to pay for all the extra pet food? He got out of bed and switched on his desk light. According to his figures, it would take until October to earn all the money he needed. Oliver picked up his stuffed owl and looked at it for a long time.

Oliver sighed and crawled back into bed. Maybe if he just went to sleep, his problems would disappear by the morning.

As soon as he woke up, Oliver gave Matthew a call.

'Big trouble,' said Oliver. He told Matthew what had happened to his mother's bicycle. Then he mentioned the latest litter of gerbils. 'Any suggestions?' Oliver asked.

Matthew thought for a long time. 'Have you got anything valuable you could sell?' he said finally.

Oliver looked around his room. 'Just my pet-care books.'

'No good,' said Matthew. 'Used books don't sell that well.'

The boys thought a bit more. 'Maybe you could get someone to lend you the money,' suggested Matthew. 'Who do you know who gets a lot of pocket-money?'

'No one,' replied Oliver. 'Except maybe Jennifer.'

'Perfect!' Matthew said. 'Phone her.'

Oliver made a face. 'There must be another way. Can't we think of anything else?' he asked.

'How much do you want to keep your owl?' Matthew said.

Oliver sighed. 'I'll ring her right away.'

When Jennifer answered the phone, Oliver could hardly hear her. She was listening to a record by her favourite rock group, the Purple Worms.

'Can you turn down the volume?' Oliver shouted. 'I can't hear you.'

'OK,' said Jennifer. A moment later she was back on the phone. 'How's that?'

'Much better,' said Oliver. He paused for a moment, trying to think of how to ask her for a loan.

'How have you been?' he began.

'Fabulous,' Jennifer replied. 'I'm having a fabulous summer. I just got back from Kim's lake-side house. We went swimming every day. She has a fabulous dock with a diving board. And you should see my tan! It's —'

'Fabulous, right?' said Oliver politely.

'How did you know?' asked Jennifer.

'Never mind,' said Oliver. He took a deep breath. 'So what else is new?'

'My turntable and speaker system,' Jennifer replied.

Oliver's heart sank. 'What turntable?' he said.

'I got a three-month advance on my pocket-money to buy a real stereo system,' Jennifer said. 'You should hear how much better my albums sound.'

'Great,' Oliver said glumly.

'Come over any time,' Jennifer said. 'It's like listening to a live concert.'

Oliver put down the phone. He sat at his desk for a long time. Finally, he pulled an old cardboard box out of his cupboard. He wrapped the owl carefully in paper towels and old newspapers, then packed it in the box. 'Bye, owl,' said Oliver sadly. 'Looks as if there's no other way out of this.'

Oliver started to walk as slowly as he could up Sutherland Avenue. He heard someone calling his name.

Oliver looked around. It was a teenage boy. Oliver remembered seeing him around.

'Oliver?' the boy said. 'I'm Tom Christopher. Parnell Williams told me about you.' Parnell was Kim's older brother.

'He said that you take care of pets,' Tom said.

'That's right,' Oliver replied. He put down the cardboard box.

'What do you know about rhesus monkeys?' Tom asked.

Oliver had just finished reading about rhesus monkeys in a book called *Animals of India*. 'Lots,' he said. 'They're one of my specialities.'

'Great!' Tom smiled. 'Parnell told me I could trust you to take good care of Zippy. That's my monkey's name.'

Oliver did some quick calculations. He might be able to get back his mother's bike and still save his stuffed owl. 'Monkeys are a lot of hard work,' said Oliver. 'I'd have to charge you about three times my usual amount.'

'That's OK,' Tom replied. 'I'd rather know he's being well taken care of.'

'How long will you be away?' Oliver asked.

'Three weeks,' Tom replied. 'We leave tomorrow.'

Oliver pretended to frown. 'Three weeks is a long time,' he said. 'And monkeys eat a lot. Do you think you could pay me the whole amount in advance?'

'I'll be back this afternoon with the money and Zippy,' said Tom.

He and Oliver shook hands. 'It's a deal,' Oliver said happily.

Oliver was in the back garden with Hopkins and Andrew when Tom arrived. Tom was pulling an enormous cage on a little red wagon. Zippy sat inside the cage on a large sleeping shelf, staring out at everyone.

'It's a gorilla!' Andrew screamed. He started to run home, but Oliver grabbed him.

'Slow down,' said Oliver. 'Is that any way to say hello to our new guest?'

Andrew looked amazed. 'It's staying with us in the garage?' he asked.

Oliver nodded. 'Remember your promise?'

'Wow,' said Andrew. 'A gorilla in the garage!' He ran off happily.

'Let me help,' said Oliver to Tom. He took the wagon handle and pulled the load into the garage. The cage was nearly big enough for Oliver to walk around in. The monkey watched Oliver carefully.

'Hi, Zippy,' said Oliver.

Zippy reached through the bars and grabbed Oliver's T-shirt. Oliver laughed. 'He likes me,' he said.

Zippy pulled harder. Oliver could feel his T-shirt start to rip. 'Hey,' Oliver cried, 'what do you think you're doing?'

Now Zippy started to laugh.

'No, no, Zippy,' said Tom. Zippy let go. 'He's testing you,' Tom said.

'No problem,' said Oliver. He looked down at the tear in his shirt.

Tom looked around the garage. 'There are a lot of animals in here,' he said. 'You must really know what you're doing.'

Oliver smiled. 'Why don't we put Zippy over in the corner, away from the door?' he said. As he and Tom set up the cage, Oliver asked a few more questions. 'Does Zippy make much noise?' he said. 'This is a very quiet area.'

'He makes a noise only if something upsets him,' Tom replied.

'I'm sure he'll be fine, then,' said Oliver.

Tom gave Oliver feeding instructions and a blanket to cover Zippy's cage at night. Before he left, he paid Oliver in advance. Oliver counted the money and stuck it into his pocket. 'Thanks, Tom,' he said. 'Zippy is in good hands.'

*

Rusty was hunched over an old car when Oliver walked into his garage. 'Come to bring me that owl?' Rusty smirked.

Oliver threw the money on the floor. 'You have one week to return the bike, Rusty,' he said.

That evening while Mrs Moffitt was having a shower, Oliver made Zippy a special supper of potatoes, apples and tomatoes. Tomorrow he would go to the Quick Shoppe to stock up on supplies. Oliver planned to keep Zippy's food out in the garage so his mother wouldn't notice it.

Oliver slipped quietly out to the garage. 'Suppertime,' he called softly. Zippy sat huddled on the corner of his sleeping shelf. He hardly looked up when Oliver placed his food in the bottom of the cage.

'I'll come back to visit you later,' Oliver told him. 'You look a little homesick to me.' Zippy kept his face turned to the wall.

Mrs Moffitt was in the kitchen starting to cook supper. 'How are those gerbils doing?' she asked.

'Fine, Mum,' Oliver replied. 'They really love that garage.'

She popped some hamburger rolls into the toaster. 'And have you found my bicycle yet?'

'No problem,' Oliver replied. 'It's in the very back

of the garage, though. It will take me about a week to get to it.'

Mrs Moffitt put some hamburger meat on to a saucer. 'Have you seen Pom-pom?' she asked.

Oliver shook his head. 'Not since you got home,' he said. 'I thought –'

His words were cut off by a horrible screech.

'What's that terrible noise?' said Mrs Moffitt. 'It sounds as if it's coming from the garage.'

Oliver gulped. 'Maybe it's Andrew,' he replied.

Mrs Moffitt opened the kitchen door and ran outside. 'Andrew? Is that you?' she called.

She was answered by another loud screech.

'It sounds as though someone is hurt,' said Mrs Moffitt. She headed for the garage.

Oliver grabbed her arm. 'You stay here, Mum,' he said. 'Sometimes Andrew likes to fool about. Let me look.'

The noise was getting louder. Oliver ran as fast as he could to the garage. When he got there, he could see Zippy clinging to the top bars of his cage. He was shrieking and pointing at something on the floor.

Oliver looked down. 'Pom-pom!' he exclaimed. 'What are you doing in there?'

Pom-pom had managed to squeeze through the bottom bars of the cage. He looked at Oliver and

quickly finished the last bite of Zippy's dinner. Zippy pointed at Pom-pom and shrieked again.

'You get out of there right now,' Oliver said.

Pom-pom looked up and growled. A piece of potato hung out of the corner of his mouth.

'Oliver, what is going on?' called Mrs Moffitt.

All the other animals began to stir now.

'Nothing, Mum,' Oliver called.

He could hear his mother coming closer.

'Is Pom-pom with you?' she demanded. Her footsteps were even closer now.

Oliver opened the cage door, grabbed Pom-pom and slammed the cage door shut. 'Move!' he hissed. Pom-pom snarled.

Oliver ran outside and shut the garage door behind him just as Mrs Moffitt walked up.

'Pom-pom!' she exclaimed. 'Was that you making all that noise?'

'He got locked in the garage somehow,' Oliver said. 'He must have been really scared.'

Mrs Moffitt took Pom-pom in her arms and gave him a big kiss. 'You poor thing,' she said. 'I've never heard you make such a frightful noise.' Pom-pom looked at the garage door and wagged his tail.

'Let's go inside,' said Mrs Moffitt. She put Pom-pom down, and he ran back over to the garage.

'*Yap, yap, yap!*' Pom-pom scratched on the door.

Oliver picked him up. 'Shouldn't you be in the house, Pom-pom?' he said.

Pom-pom sat next to the kitchen door for the rest of the evening. 'That's odd,' said Mrs Moffitt. 'I think he wants to go back out to the garage.'

Oliver shook his head. 'Strangest thing I ever saw,' he said. 'Why would he want to do that?'

When Oliver had finished washing the dishes, he phoned Matthew. 'Other than the close call with Pom-pom, everything is working out perfectly,' he said. 'I can't wait until we go to the beach.'

'Great,' said Matthew. 'Oh, I meant to ask. Who's going to look after all the animals while you're away?'

'Look after the . . . Oh, no!' said Oliver. 'I was so busy getting the bike back, I forgot all about that!'

'Couldn't Andrew do it?' suggested Matthew. 'He knows the whole routine now.'

'He's not very good in emergencies,' said Oliver. 'I'd like to find someone more responsible.' He thought for a moment. 'How about *you*, Matthew?'

'Can't,' Matthew said. 'We're going away that week for a Farley family reunion.'

'What's that?' asked Oliver.

'It's when you meet all these relatives you've never met before,' Matthew explained. 'It's mostly grown-ups.'

Oliver sighed. 'That leaves just one person who can do it,' he said. 'Jennifer.'

'Do you think she can handle it?' Matthew asked.

Oliver shook his head slowly. 'I don't know,' he said. 'She hates gerbils. I don't think she's going to like the idea.'

'Wait,' said Matthew. 'Maybe there's a way to convince her. I think I might have a good idea.'

# CHAPTER
## 4

Oliver knocked on Jennifer's door that afternoon. Jennifer answered, wearing a bathing suit, beach robe and sunglasses.

'Are you going swimming?' Oliver asked.

'Sunbathing in the garden,' Jennifer replied. 'I don't want to lose my fabulous tan.'

'Right,' said Oliver.

He and Jennifer went out to the garden and drank lemonade.

'How's your summer been, Oliver?' she asked.

Oliver took a deep breath. 'Great,' he said. 'But I need to ask a small favour.'

Jennifer nodded.

'How would you like to take care of Pom-pom for a week?' Oliver asked. 'Mum and I are going to the beach for a holiday.'

'I'd love to!' Jennifer exclaimed. 'Pom-pom is so sweet. Can he stay here with me?'

'I think he'd be more comfortable at my house,' Oliver replied. Jennifer's cat, Princess Fluffy, had stayed at Oliver's once for several weeks. Fluffy and Pom-pom couldn't stand each other.

'Besides,' Oliver continued, 'I need you to watch the gerbils and a few other things.'

'Ugh,' said Jennifer. 'I forgot about those gerbils. Count me out.'

Oliver reached into his pocket. 'Before you say no,' he said, 'I'd like to offer you these as a thank-you.' He held out two tickets.

Jennifer looked at the tickets and screamed. 'I don't believe it!' she said. 'Tickets to the Purple Worms concert! How did you ever get them? It's been sold out for months.'

Oliver smiled knowingly. 'Special connections,' he said. He held them out for Jennifer to inspect.

'Fifth row, centre,' she shrieked. Jennifer reached over to hug Oliver, who managed to duck just in time.

Oliver put the tickets back into his pocket. 'You realize,' he said, 'that you need to help me out to get the tickets.'

'Absolutely,' Jennifer said. 'I'll take care of *fourteen* gerbils if you want.'

Oliver took one last sip of lemonade. 'Perfect.' He smiled. 'Be at my house this afternoon at three. I'll show you the whole routine.'

Matthew stopped by at noon on his way to karate class. 'How did it go?' he asked.

'No problem,' Oliver replied, 'once Jennifer saw the Purple Worms tickets.'

'I still can't believe I won those tickets in a record-shop raffle,' Matthew said. 'Can I meet Zippy now?'

'Of course,' said Oliver. 'Andrew has just finished cleaning the cage.'

Zippy was eating a banana and chattering to Andrew. 'I think he's getting over his homesickness,' Oliver said.

When Zippy saw Oliver, he threw his banana down and ran to the side of the cage. Oliver unlocked the door and took Zippy by the hand.

'This is Matthew,' Oliver said.

Zippy grabbed Matthew's T-shirt. 'That means he likes you,' Oliver explained.

'Does Jennifer know about the other animals?' asked Matthew. Zippy was still clinging to Matthew's shirt.

'Not yet,' Oliver replied. 'She'll find out this afternoon.'

Jennifer showed up at three on the dot. 'I'm ready,' she said. 'Take me to those gerbils.'

'Why don't we say hello to Pom-pom first?' Oliver suggested. 'I know he can't wait to see you.'

Jennifer gave Pom-pom a big kiss. Pom-pom licked Jennifer's face and wagged his tail. 'We're going to have lots of fun together,' she said.

Oliver explained Pom-pom's feeding and walking schedule.

'Can I take him to the Quick Shoppe?' Jennifer asked.

'I suppose so,' said Oliver. He put the dog in the kitchen and made sure the door was closed. 'Now let's go and see the gerbils,' he said.

Andrew was waiting outside the garage door. 'This is my assistant,' Oliver explained. 'He'll be glad to answer any questions and help you out.'

'Aren't you a sweet little boy?' Jennifer said. She gave him a kiss on the forehead.

'Yuk,' said Andrew.

'Why don't we look around the garage?' Oliver said. He signalled Andrew to be quiet.

It took a moment for Jennifer's eyes to adjust to the dark garage. 'Eeek!' she screamed. 'What's that ape doing in here?'

Zippy pointed at Jennifer and screamed back.

'That's a rhesus monkey,' Oliver said. 'He won't hurt you.'

Jennifer walked over to Zippy's cage and took a closer look. 'He's quite sweet,' she said. 'Do you ever dress him up?'

Oliver was beginning to wonder if he'd made a big mistake.

Zippy reached out and grabbed Jennifer's hair.

'Ouch!' she yelled. Zippy pulled harder.

'No, no,' Oliver said.

'Stop it, you horrible monkey!' Jennifer yelled.

Zippy began to laugh.

'Do something!' Jennifer shrieked. 'He's pulling all my hair out!'

Oliver stood helplessly next to the cage. 'No, no, Zippy,' he said again.

Suddenly Andrew appeared on the other side of the garage. He was carrying a large bucket of water. *Ker-splash!* In one second Jennifer, Zippy and Oliver were drenched. Zippy let go.

'Ugggh,' said Jennifer. She felt the top of her head to make sure her hair was still there.

Andrew clapped his hands together. 'That stopped him,' he said. He shook his finger at Zippy. 'Bad monkey.'

Zippy crawled on to his sleeping shelf and turned his face to the wall.

'Are you OK?' Oliver asked Jennifer.

'I suppose so.' She sniffed. She wrung out her shirt and slowly took a look around the garage. 'Isn't that Hopkins?' she said. 'I thought he was staying with Kim's next-door neighbour.' She walked past the tropical fish tanks and over to the guinea pigs' cage. Next to the guinea pigs were three cages of gerbils. 'I don't believe this,' Jennifer gasped. 'How many animals do you have in here?'

Oliver thought for a minute. 'Not including the two fish tanks, only about twenty,' he replied.

Jennifer threw her hands into the air. 'I hope you don't expect me to take care of all of them,' she said. 'I agreed to take care of Pom-pom and the gerbils.'

Oliver pulled the concert tickets out of his pocket. 'I'd hate to see these go to waste,' he said.

'Not fair!' Jennifer shouted. 'That's blackmail, Oliver.'

Oliver shrugged. 'That's my offer,' he said. 'Take it or leave it.'

Jennifer sighed. 'OK, OK,' she replied. 'I suppose it's not too much to ask. But, first, would you mind telling me what's going on?'

It took Jennifer a long time to learn the routine. 'Some of the things these animals eat are disgusting,' she said. Oliver was showing her how to feed freeze-dried worms to the tropical fish.

'Don't worry,' Oliver told her. 'Andrew will help you with the nasty bits.'

Andrew was playing with a clump of worms on the palm of his hand. 'Nice wormy,' he said.

Jennifer shuddered.

'The most important thing,' Oliver continued, 'is that you come here at least three times a day.'

Jennifer sighed once more. 'If the Purple Worms only knew the sacrifices I made to see them . . .'

Oliver smiled. 'Don't worry, Jennifer,' he said. 'Everything is going to work out perfectly.'

Rusty returned Mrs Moffitt's bike two days later. 'Just in time,' Oliver said. He took it on a test run to make sure it worked properly.

'What a smooth ride,' Oliver exclaimed. 'Thanks, Rusty.'

'Don't thank me,' Rusty replied. 'You're the one who's had to pay for it.'

Before Oliver could reply, Rusty was half-way down the street.

Oliver shrugged. At least he'd got the bicycle back. Now he could really look forward to his holiday. Oliver went up to his room and looked over his budget sheet. All the animals were due to be collected the day after he returned. 'Not bad,' he said to himself.

Oliver remembered the locket. Well, at least Mum is getting a nice holiday, he thought.

That night, Oliver was too excited to sleep. He and his mother were leaving for the seaside in the morning. Oliver sat up in bed to make sure his packed suitcase was still sitting by the door. Had he remembered everything? Did Jennifer have all her instructions? Would the animals be all right? Oliver hoped so. He wanted this to be the best holiday ever.

*

'Welcome to the Whaler's Inn,' said the woman at the reception desk. 'You'll be staying in the Captain's Room. It's the second door on your left, straight down the hall.'

Oliver grabbed his suitcase and raced ahead. The Captain's Room overlooked the sea. It had a large screened porch and two double beds. On the wall hung a huge oil portrait labelled CAPTAIN HORATIO. Oliver wondered if the Whaler's Inn had once belonged to Captain Horatio.

Oliver glanced around the room for the telephone. He noticed it in the corner by the bed. 'I'll have to phone Jennifer tonight,' he reminded himself.

Oliver had already changed into his bathing suit by the time his mother arrived.

'That was fast,' she said with a smile.

'Come on, Mum,' Oliver called. 'Let's go to the beach!'


Oliver phoned Jennifer that evening when his mother was in the shower. 'How's it going?' he asked.

'I can't find the rabbit food,' Jennifer answered.

'It's the same as the guinea pig food,' Oliver said.

'Oh, that's right,' said Jennifer. 'In the large coffee tin.' She sighed. 'There's so much to remember.'

'Ask Andrew to help you,' Oliver said. 'He knows the whole routine.'

'How's the beach?' Jennifer asked. 'Are you getting a nice tan?'

'It's great,' said Oliver. 'The waves are really high. We went swimming all afternoon, then we went for a bike ride. We had lobster for dinner.'

'*Real* lobster with the claws and eyes and insides showing?' asked Jennifer.

'Mum says it's a delicacy,' Oliver replied.

'Horrible,' said Jennifer. 'How can you eat that poor little lobster and still call yourself an animal lover?'

'You eat fish or meat sometimes, don't you?'

'That's different,' said Jennifer. 'I don't have to look at the eyes or the insides.'

Oliver just rolled his eyes.

'I've got to go now,' Jennifer said. 'It's time for *Lace Curtains* on TV.'

'Your mum lets you watch that rubbish?' Oliver said.

'Of course,' Jennifer replied. 'Doesn't yours?'

Oliver worried all night about the animals. What if Jennifer got the pet food mixed up? What if she decided to leave in the middle of feeding to go and watch *Lace Curtains*? What if she forgot about the animals completely? Oliver decided he'd phone every day to make sure. It would cost him some extra money, but he didn't want to take any chances.

'You've been spending a lot of time on the telephone,' Mrs Moffitt remarked several days later. 'Is Jennifer having trouble?'

'No problem, Mum,' Oliver replied. 'I just want to make sure she's taking good care of Pom-pom. You know how temperamental he can get.'

'Absolutely,' said Mrs Moffitt. 'In fact, why don't you let me speak to Jennifer the next time? You always seem to call when I'm in the shower.'

'Right,' said Oliver. 'I'll remember that.'

Oliver spread his shell collection across the porch. He began sorting them by colour.

'Do you know the names of all those shells?' asked Mrs Moffitt.

'Not yet,' Oliver replied. 'I'm using this book to help me.'

Mrs Moffitt peered at the floor. 'Is that black-and-brown shell moving?' she asked.

Oliver picked up the cone-shaped culprit and looked inside. 'Yep,' he said. 'There's a hermit crab in there.' He held it up for Mrs Moffitt to inspect. 'When he outgrows this shell, he'll move on to another home.'

'I hope you don't bring him to *our* home,' said Mrs

Moffitt. The phone rang. 'I'll answer it.' She stepped inside.

Oliver could hear his mother talking to someone and laughing. A few minutes later, she came out to the porch. 'It's Jennifer.'

Oliver raced to the other room. 'What's happened?' he shouted into the phone.

'Relax,' said Jennifer. 'I've just run out of dog food.'

'You didn't mention the other pets to Mum, did you?' Oliver whispered.

'What?' said Jennifer.

Mrs Moffitt walked into the room.

'I said, why didn't you mention it sooner?' said Oliver.

'Mention *what* sooner?' Jennifer asked.

Oliver looked over at his mother and smiled. 'Just give him that leftover package of sausage tomorrow,' he told Jennifer. 'We'll be home the next day.'

'Give *who* the sausage?' Jennifer said. 'Pom-pom?'

'Right,' said Oliver.

'But what shall I give Zippy?' Jennifer asked.

Mrs Moffitt sat down on the bed and started to paint her toenails. 'Thank her for all the nice help she's giving us,' Mrs Moffitt whispered.

Oliver nodded. 'My mother, who is sitting right

here next to me on the bed, wants to thank you,' he said.

Mrs Moffitt gave Oliver a funny look.

'Oh, I get it!' said Jennifer. 'Your mother doesn't know anything about this.'

'*Right*,' Oliver said.

'So what do I feed Zippy?' she asked.

'Don't ask me,' Oliver shouted. '*You* work it out!'

Mrs Moffitt looked up. 'Oliver!' she said. 'Why are you being so rude to Jennifer?'

'Give him some chopped bananas and apples,' Oliver said in a low voice.

Mrs Moffitt shook her head. 'I hope you aren't telling Jennifer to give Pom-pom all that fruit. You know what it does to his stomach.'

Oliver sighed. 'Never mind, Jennifer,' he said. 'I'll leave it up to your good judgement. We'll see you in two days.'

'But I don't understand –' Jennifer said.

Oliver hung up the phone.

The next day was Oliver's last at the beach. He spent so much time in the sea that his mother told him he was beginning to look like a prune. At noon Oliver and his mother went to their favourite restaurant, Davy Jones's Luncheonette.

'I wish we didn't have to go home,' Oliver sighed as he finished his lobster roll.

'Me too,' said Mrs Moffitt. 'Wouldn't it be nice to spend all summer in a place like this?'

'Yes,' said Oliver with a sigh. He thought about all the dogs and cats he'd seen here. He could probably do great business. 'What time do we have to leave tomorrow?' he asked.

'I'd like to start as early as possible,' said Mrs Moffitt. 'Do you think you can help me tie the bicycles on the car roof again?'

'Sure,' said Oliver. He wondered how Jennifer was getting on. He decided not to ring her again until they got home. Everything is probably fine, he thought. No problem.

Oliver and his mother pulled into their driveway at noon. Oliver was relieved to see the garage still standing. So far, so good, he thought. Oliver hopped out of the car and climbed on to the roof. 'Might as well start with the bikes,' he told his mother.

There was a loud scream.

'That came from the garage,' Mrs Moffitt said. She and Oliver looked over and saw Pom-pom run out of the garage, spin in a circle and run back inside.

There were more screams.

'I'll see what it is, Mum,' Oliver said.

By the time Oliver had climbed off the car roof, his mother was half-way across the garden. Before Oliver could reach her, Mrs Moffitt pushed the garage door open. 'What is going on here?' she gasped.

'It's not my fault,' Jennifer screamed from the top of the chest of drawers. 'Look what that horrible monkey has done. He let all those disgusting gerbils and guinea pigs loose!'

Animals were everywhere. Overturned tins of pet food lay strewn across the floor. In one corner Pompom was trying to catch a guinea pig that had wedged itself under the chest of drawers. As Hopkins chewed on a wooden table leg, Zippy gleefully tore open another bag of rabbit food and tossed it into the fish tank. Andrew stood next to the chest of drawers holding an empty gerbil cage and crying. 'I want my mummy,' he wailed. 'I can't catch all these gerbils by myself.'

As Mrs Moffitt looked around the garage, her face turned white, then red, then purple. Oliver wished he could sink into the floor and disappear. Finally, she grabbed hold of his arm and led Oliver out into the yard. 'All right, young man,' she said. 'Start talking. You've got a lot of explaining to do.'

# CHAPTER
## 5

Mrs Moffitt was not pleased. No matter how Oliver tried to explain, his mother didn't like his answers.

'But, Mum,' Oliver said, 'all the animals except the gerbils and guinea pigs are due to be picked up tomorrow.'

'That still doesn't excuse what you did,' said Mrs Moffitt. 'Besides, what do you plan to do with the extra gerbils and the guinea pigs?'

Oliver thought for a moment. 'We'll have a lawn sale,' he said. 'I'll sell all that old garage furniture and the guinea pigs at the same time. The gerbils will go back to school with me next week. I'm sure Mr Thompson won't mind a few extra gerbils.'

Another scream came from the garage. Mrs Moffitt shook her head and sighed. 'Why don't you go and check on Jennifer and Andrew? It sounds as if they could use your help. We'll continue this discussion later.'

Jennifer was still directing traffic from the top of

the chest of drawers. 'Did you get into trouble?' she asked Oliver.

'What do *you* think?' answered Oliver. He reached down and grabbed a baby gerbil as it ran across his foot.

'Well, don't blame *me*,' said Jennifer. 'It was *your* idea to take in all these stupid pets in the first place.'

Zippy pointed his finger at Oliver and laughed.

'Oh, shut up, Zippy,' said Oliver. 'No one asked your opinion.'

Oliver sat at the supper table and pushed his food around with a fork. He'd spent all day cleaning up the garage.

'You haven't said a word since we sat down,' said Mrs Moffitt.

'I know,' Oliver replied. He mixed his cottage pie into a gooey heap.

'Did you get everything sorted out in the garage?' asked Mrs Moffitt.

'Yes,' said Oliver. 'That Zippy certainly knows how to make a mess.' He sighed and took a bite of his food.

'Oliver,' said his mother, 'why didn't you tell me about all those animals?'

'Because I didn't think you'd let me keep them,'

Oliver answered. He decided not to mention the locket.

'I might have considered it,' she said.

'But you said only one pet at a time,' Oliver protested. 'I thought I'd get into trouble.'

'You're in bigger trouble now.'

Oliver sighed again. How was he ever going to make up for this?

Mrs Moffitt looked at Oliver. 'I've been thinking about what you said about a lawn sale,' she said. 'Why don't we go to the garage after supper and have a look at what's out there?'

Oliver looked up from his plate. 'Mum,' he said, 'I promise I'll make it up to you. The garage is going to be the cleanest you've ever seen it. I'll find homes for all those guinea pigs too.'

Mrs Moffitt nodded. 'I hope so,' she said.


Oliver was up early the next morning. After he had fed all the pets, he dragged the sofa out on to the lawn. Next to it he put the chest of drawers. Several cars slowed down as they drove past.

'Come on over,' Oliver shouted. 'Lawn sale today.'

Mrs Moffitt stuck her head out of the bedroom window. 'Oliver!' she cried. 'What in the world are you doing? It's six thirty in the morning!'

'It's O K, Mum,' said Oliver. 'I'm getting ready for the lawn sale.'

A man in a pick-up truck pulled up. 'Is that sofa for sale?' he asked. Oliver looked up at his mother and grinned. 'It certainly is,' he said. 'Would you like a nice baby guinea pig to go along with it?'

The man scratched his head. 'A what?' he asked.

'Never mind,' said Oliver. 'Let me show you that sofa.'

By the time Mrs Moffitt was ready to leave for work, Oliver had sold the sofa, a plant pot and two lamps. 'Keep up the good work,' she told him.

'I will, Mum,' said Oliver. 'When you get home tonight, the garage will be empty.'

A few minutes later Kim appeared. 'Hi, Oliver,' she said.

'Hi, Kim. How was your holiday?'

'Fabulous,' she replied. 'Did Hopkins behave?'

'He was a perfect guest,' Oliver said.

Kim looked around the yard. 'What's going on here?' she asked.

'We're having a lawn sale!' Andrew appeared from behind the chest of drawers.

'This is my assistant,' Oliver explained. 'We're selling a few things from the garage.'

'Would you like a guinea pig?' Andrew asked. He pulled one out of the box for Kim to inspect.

'Those are adorable,' Kim said. 'Where did they come from?'

'Someone bananad them,' Andrew said.

'He means *abandoned*,' Oliver explained.

'Ohhh, the poor things,' said Kim. 'We used to have guinea pigs. Maybe my mum wouldn't mind a few again.'

'Are you sure?' Oliver asked.

'May I use your phone to ring my mum?' said Kim.

'Of course,' said Oliver. He turned to Andrew and smiled. 'See?' he said. 'This is going to be easy.'

By noon, Oliver had sold a chipped vase and a lawn-mower that didn't work. Kim had taken Hopkins and two of the guinea pigs. Oliver looked around the garden. 'There's still a lot of stuff here,' he told Andrew. 'Maybe you can stand near the street and try to flag more cars down.'

Andrew headed for the pavement.

'Wait,' said Oliver. 'I've got a better idea.' He ran into the house and came out with scissors, a ball of string and an old red scarf that belonged to his mother. 'Now get the sign we made this morning.'

Andrew picked up the big piece of cardboard with the words: LAWN SALE TODAY. GREAT DEALS ON FURNITURE, ODDS 'N' ENDS AND GUINEA PIGS.

Oliver used the scissors to poke two holes in the sign, and a piece of string to hang it around Andrew's neck. The sign reached down to Andrew's knees. Oliver handed Andrew the long red scarf.

'As the cars drive by, wave the scarf and shout, "Lawn Sale!"' Oliver told Andrew. 'You're sure to attract attention.'

'OK, Oliver,' said Andrew. He waddled off to the pavement. A few minutes later an old green estate car pulled up.

'Got anything good here?' the man asked cheerfully as he got out.

Oliver jumped to his feet. 'Yes, sir,' he replied. 'Some beautiful antique furniture and a couple of friendly guinea pigs.'

'Guinea pigs?' said the man. He looked around the lawn. 'I was thinking more of furniture.'

The man's wife was already standing next to the chest of drawers. 'David, look,' she said. 'This is perfect.'

The man pulled a tape measure out of his pocket. 'We've just moved from a flat to a house,' he explained. 'We're really short of furniture.'

'This is a fine chest of drawers,' Oliver said. He opened the top drawer. 'Look at that construction.'

The man peered into the drawer. 'Nice,' he observed.

Two more cars pulled up. 'Andrew,' Oliver called, 'come and talk to these people while I go and help the new customers.' Andrew nodded and ran over as best he could.

Four small children got out of the first car and

rushed to the guinea pig box. 'Daddy, look!' shouted the tallest child. 'This one looks just like Winkie.'

The child's father came up to Oliver. 'Our guinea pig died last week,' he explained.

The smallest boy picked the guinea pig up by the neck. 'Nice Winkie,' he said. 'Good piggy.'

'Mike, be careful,' said the tallest girl. She snatched the guinea pig away from him. 'We'll take this one,' she told Oliver.

'Fine,' said Oliver. Out of the corner of his eye he could see the young couple moving the chest of drawers to their car. Andrew was chattering away.

'Can you change a tenner?' said the man buying the guinea pig.

'I'll have to get it from upstairs,' Oliver said. He noticed Tom Christopher walking up the driveway. 'Hi, Tom,' Oliver shouted. 'I'll be with you in a minute. Zippy's in the garage.'

Tom waved and disappeared into the garage. Several more cars had stopped now.

'Andrew!' Oliver shouted. 'I need your help.' Andrew nodded and kept talking to the couple with the chest of drawers.

'Wait here,' Oliver told the man. 'I'll be back in a minute with your change.'

By the time Oliver returned, the young couple had left. Tom had already loaded Zippy's cage on to the red wagon. The four small children were trying to poke their fingers through the bars.

'Stand back,' Tom was saying. 'He'll grab you if you're not careful.'

'Need some help?'

Oliver spun around. 'Sam!' he said. 'When did you get home?'

'Just now.' Sam grinned. She looked around the lawn. 'Looks as if you've got your hands full.'

'I'll explain it all later,' Oliver said. 'I'm glad you're back.'

Late that afternoon Sam, Oliver and Andrew sat on the front lawn drinking lemonade. 'What a day!' Oliver said. 'I can't believe we sold everything.'

'Even the guinea pigs,' Andrew added.

'It got pretty crazy for a while,' Sam said. She took a long sip of lemonade, then blew a few bubbles through her straw. 'Tim B. was surprised to get back *two* aquariums.'

'And twenty more fish,' said Oliver.

'I still don't understand why you took in all those extra pets,' Sam said.

'It all started with that locket,' Oliver answered. 'I thought that if I took in an extra customer, I'd earn enough money to buy the locket for Mum's birthday. All I ended up with was trouble, though.'

'You were going to buy your mummy a rocket?' said Andrew.

'No, a *locket*,' Oliver said.

'Oh. What's a locket?'

'It's an old-fashioned necklace,' Oliver replied. 'Mum lost one a long time ago. I wanted to buy another one just like it from the antique shop.'

Andrew pulled a clump of grass out of the lawn and dropped it into his empty lemonade glass. 'Did it look like a heart?' he asked.

Oliver sat up. 'Yes, it did. How did you know?'

'Because there was a locket that looked like a heart in the garage,' Andrew replied.

'There was?' Oliver said. 'Where?'

Andrew thought for a minute. 'In the chest of drawers,' he said.

Oliver groaned. '*Now* you tell me!' he said. 'That was sold hours ago.'

'Maybe we can find the owners,' said Sam. 'Your mum is sure to forgive you once she sees the locket.'

'You're probably right,' Oliver said. 'But where will we ever find those people?'

'Do you remember anything about them?' asked Sam. 'Their car? Where they live?'

'I was so busy then,' Oliver sighed.

'They had a green car,' Andrew volunteered.

'That's right!' Oliver said. 'Now I remember. They

had just moved from a flat to a house. Andrew, did they tell you anything else? You talked to them for a long time.'

Andrew squeezed his eyes shut. 'I think their name was Smith.'

Oliver groaned again. 'There must be a million Smiths in the telephone book,' he said. 'We'll never find them.'

'They live on Adams Road,' Andrew continued. 'They have a kitty named Pumpkin.'

'Perfect,' said Oliver. 'Adams Road is really close to here.'

'Why don't we ride our bikes over there and try to find them?' said Sam.

'Can't hurt,' Oliver replied. He patted Andrew on the back. 'Thanks, Andrew,' he said. 'Maybe Mum will forgive me after all.'

Sam and Oliver quickly finished their lemonade, took Andrew home to his mother and raced over to Adams Road. 'Now what?' said Sam.

'Easy,' Oliver replied. 'We just start looking for an old green estate car.'

Oliver and Sam slowly rode their bikes up one side of the street and down the other. 'I don't see anything,' said Sam.

'They're probably still out,' Oliver said. 'Let's just wait a while.'

A long time passed.

'Maybe we should try something else,' Sam decided. 'I'm going to knock on a few doors.' She walked over to a white house with black shutters. A woman wearing a dressing-gown and curlers answered the door.

'Excuse me,' said Sam, 'but we're looking for the Smith family. They've just moved into this street.'

The woman shook her head. 'Never heard of them,' she said. She closed the door in Sam's face.

'Let's try the next house,' said Oliver.

A man with a big pot belly opened the door. 'It's the paper boy,' he called.

'No, I'm –' said Oliver.

But the man had already disappeared. A few seconds later, a woman came to the door. 'You're not the paper boy,' she said.

'I know,' said Oliver. 'We're trying to –'

'No more magazine subscriptions,' said the woman. Before Oliver could say anything else, she shut the door.

'Remind me never to trick-or-treat in this street,' Oliver muttered. He and Sam tried several more doors without success.

'I don't understand it,' Oliver said. 'No one on Adams Road has ever heard of the Smith family.'

'Maybe we should give up,' said Sam.

'No,' Oliver replied stubbornly. 'I want Mum to

have that locket. They've got to be here somewhere.'
Oliver watched several cars drive past. Suddenly he pointed and yelled. 'It's them!' he shouted. 'In the green car!'

'Where?' said Sam.

'There!' Oliver ran to the street. A green estate car whizzed by. 'Stop!' Oliver shouted. 'Slow down!'

Sam hopped on to her bike. 'Come on,' she said. 'Let's try to catch them.'

'Are you crazy?' said Oliver. 'That car is already at the end of the street.'

Sam cut across a large field. 'Hurry up, slowcoach,' she yelled. 'I know a short cut.'

Oliver had never gone this way before. 'Slow down, Sam,' he called. 'I'm going to lose you.'

He didn't notice the large hole in the path until it was too late. Bang! Oliver went flying. Then the ground came rushing up.

'Oliver are you O K?'

Oliver raised his eyes and saw Sam's shoes standing in front of him. 'Yes. I just didn't see that hole.' He stood up and put his hand to his head. 'I just . . . ow!' He took his hand away quickly.

'Looks as if you're growing a big lump there,' Sam said.

'Never mind that,' said Oliver. 'Did the Smiths get away?'

Sam nodded. 'By the time I reached the corner, they were gone.'

Oliver carefully touched the bump on his head.

'Are you sure you're O K?' asked Sam.

'No problem,' Oliver answered. He brushed off his jeans and went to his bicycle. 'What are we going to do now?' he asked. 'Our one chance to get the locket back, and we blew it.'

'Why don't we just go home?' said Sam. 'Maybe Mr Huff still has the other locket in his antique shop. We'll work out some way to get the money.'

'Don't say that!' Oliver groaned. 'That's why I'm in all this trouble.' He climbed back on to his bike. 'How do we get out of here?'

He and Sam pedalled slowly through the field. 'It's only a short ride to Sutherland Avenue,' Sam said. They turned down a street with lots of new homes.

Oliver slowed down. The lump on his forehead felt as if it was getting bigger. 'Sam,' he called. 'I think we'd better stop for a few minutes. I'm hurting all over.'

He and Sam got off their bicycles and rested on the kerb.

'I suppose it could be worse,' Oliver said. 'I could be seeing double. Two stop signs, two driveways with white-and-red mailboxes, two green estate cars . . ' Oliver stopped talking and stared.

'Sam,' he said slowly, 'do you see a green estate car parked in that driveway?'

Sam began to grin. 'It's a green estate car, all right.' She looked at Oliver. 'And that's what we're looking for.'

Oliver nodded.

'Let's go,' Sam said.

Oliver forgot about all his aches and pains as he raced for the mailbox.

Sam read the address. 'The Adams Family, 3212 Smith Road. Wait a second,' she said. 'Weren't we looking for the Smith family on Adams Road?' She and Oliver burst out laughing.

'Shall we ring their bell?' said Oliver.

The Adamses eagerly led the way to the old chest of drawers. Oliver held his breath as he opened each drawer and looked inside. No locket in the first drawer, and none in the second. The third drawer was empty too. Could Andrew have been mistaken? Oliver wondered.

Slowly, Oliver slid out the last drawer. Hidden in the darkness at the very back was something gold and shiny.

Oliver looked up at Sam and smiled. 'I think we've just solved the mystery of Mum's missing locket!'

Oliver waited anxiously on the living-room couch. His mother was due home any minute. Pom-pom ran to the door and began barking. Here she is, Oliver thought.

'Hello, Oliver,' said Mrs Moffitt as she came through the door. 'How did everything go today?'

Oliver stood up and grinned. 'Please follow me to the garage, madam,' he said.

When they reached the garage door, Oliver turned to his mother. 'Close your eyes,' he instructed. Oliver opened the door and led his mother inside. 'Now you can open them,' he said.

'Why, Oliver,' exclaimed Mrs Moffitt, 'this place is spotless.'

'Have a look around,' said Oliver.

Mrs Moffitt slowly toured the garage. 'I don't believe how much space there is in here,' she marvelled. 'We even have room for the car.'

In the middle of the garage floor sat a small package. 'What's this?' said Mrs Moffitt. She reached down and picked up the box.

'Open it,' said Oliver.

Mrs Moffitt unwrapped the box. 'Oliver!' she exclaimed. 'It's my lost locket! Where ever did you find this?'

'Happy birthday, Mum,' said Oliver. 'I hope you'll forgive me for all the trouble I caused.'

Mrs Moffitt gave Oliver a hug. 'Oliver,' she said, 'of course I forgive you. I would have forgiven you even if you hadn't found the locket.'

'You would?' Oliver said.

'Of course,' said Mrs Moffitt. 'I think you've learned your lesson without my having to tell you.'

'I suppose you're right,' said Oliver.

Mrs Moffitt smiled. 'Oliver,' she said suddenly, 'where did you get that awful-looking bump on your forehead?'

Oliver felt the lump. 'This?' he said. 'It's nothing.' Oliver shrugged. 'I just had a small accident on my bike. It hurt for a while, but now I'm fine.'

'You let me know if it starts to bother you again,' said Mrs Moffitt.

'I don't think it will,' said Oliver. 'Something tells me that everything has turned out just fine.'

## FRYING AS USUAL
### *Joan Lingard*

Disaster strikes and Francettis when Mr Francetti breaks his leg. Their fish and chip shop never closes, but who is going to run is now that he's in hospital; and their mother is in Italy? The answer is quite simple to Toni, Rosita and Paula, and with the help of Grandpa they decide to carry on frying as usual. But it's not that easy . . .

## THE FREEDOM MACHINE
### *Joan Lingard*

Mungo dislikes Aunt Janet and to avoid staying with her he decies to hit the open road and look after himself, and with his bike he heads northwards bound for adventure and freedom. But he soon discovers that freedom isn't quite what he's expected, especially when his food supplies are stolen, and in the course of his journey he learns a few things about himself.

## KING DEATH'S GARDEN
### *Ann Halam*

Maurice has discovered a way of visiting the past, and whatever its dangers it's too exciting for him to want to give up – yet. A subtle and intriguing ghost story for older readers.

## STRAW FIRE
### *Angela Hassall*

Kevin and Sam meet Mark, an older boy who is sleeping rough up on the Heath behind their street. Kevin feels there is something weird about Mark, something he can't quite put his finger on. And he is soon to discover that there is something very frightening and dangerous about Mark too.